Christmas Eve Magic

Inspired by Charles Dickens' A Christmas Carol

For all the orphans of Christmases past, present and future — LP

Originally published under the title *Un chant de Noël*
by Dominique et compagnie
Text and illustrations © 2006 Les éditions Héritage inc.
English translation © 2006 Kids Can Press
English translation by Brigitte Shapiro

Kids Can Press acknowledges the financial support of the Government of
Ontario, through the Ontario Media Development Corporation's Ontario Book
Initiative; the Ontario Arts Council; the Canada Council for the Arts; and the
Government of Canada, through the BPIDP, for our publishing activity.

Published in Canada by
Kids Can Press Ltd.
29 Birch Avenue
Toronto, ON M4V 1E2

Published in the U.S. by
Kids Can Press Ltd.
2250 Military Road
Tonawanda, NY 14150

www.kidscanpress.com

The artwork in this book was rendered in oil on canvas.
The text is set in Bookman.

Edited by Yvette Ghione
Designed by Céleste Gagnon
Printed and bound in China

This book is smyth sewn casebound.
CM 06 0 9 8 7 6 5 4 3 2 1

Library and Archives Canada Cataloguing in Publication

Papineau, Lucie
[Chant de Noël. English]
        Christmas eve magic / written by Lucie Papineau ; illustrated
by Stéphane Poulin.

Translation of: Un chant de Noël.
Based on A Christmas carol by Charles Dickens.
ISBN-13: 978-1-55337-953-9 (bound)
ISBN-10: 1-55337-953-5 (bound)

1. Christmas stories, Canadian (English). I. Poulin, Stéphane II. Title.

PS8581.A6658C4513 2006   jC843'.54   C2005-907046-3

Kids Can Press is a corus™ Entertainment company

Christmas Eve Magic

Inspired by Charles Dickens' A Christmas Carol

Lucie Papineau

Stéphane Poulin

Kids Can Press

Long ago and far, far away, there
was a small town where, one
Christmas Eve, magic spread its
wings, warming the hearts of
everyone who lived there.

"Tra-la-la," sang the twirling snowflakes.

"Ding-a-ling," tinkled the dancing bells.

"Mmmm, yum!" exclaimed the children
in front of the pastry shop window.

Indeed, the spirit of Christmas shone
brightly in the eyes of all the children
— all except one.

In his huge mansion at the top of the hill, Barton sat
sulking. The butler, the maid and the cook would happily
have let the magic of Christmas into the house, but their
young master had shut the door on it.

Barton did not like to hear the homeless orphans caroling,
nor did he like the stars shining on the tall Christmas trees.
He didn't even like the smell of gingerbread.

Barton hated Christmas.

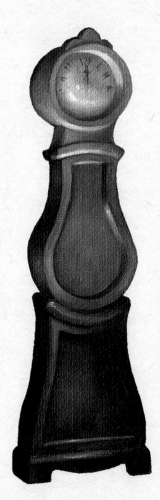

Barton sat alone in his attic room counting his toys over and over again. Once he was sure that none were missing, he closed his large safe and went to bed.

"If I fall asleep right away," he thought, "the night will pass quickly. Then one more day, and this miserable Christmas will be over."

Barton pulled up the covers and waited for sleep to come.

But Barton could not fall asleep. Although the hands on the large clock kept turning and turning, the anger in his heart kept him wide awake.

Suddenly, he saw something appear in the candlelight — a mouse dressed exactly as he was, in a nightshirt.

"You've closed your door on the magic of Christmas," the little mouse said, "but we mice have opened ours …"

At that very moment,
the twelve strokes of midnight
began to sound. *Dong. Dong.
Dong* …
　　Barton's heart seemed to
pound to the same rhythm
as he felt himself grow smaller
and smaller until he was no
bigger than the little mouse.
　　Silently, the little mouse
led him to a hole hidden
at the foot of the wall, then
through a strange maze of
secret passageways. At
the very end shone a soft,
golden light.

"Look closely," said the little mouse, "and you will see
the magic of Christmas Past."

Through the opening in the wall, Barton could see
a magnificent Christmas tree alight in all its splendor
standing in the living room of the mansion. The strains of
a violin rose in the air, together with the sparkling laughter
of a very small child.

Barton stared wide-eyed as he realized that the man
playing the violin was his father and that he was the two
year old sitting on his mother's lap. "Look how I laughed
then, how happy I was ..." whispered Barton as a ghostly
mist began to creep into the living room.

When the veil of mist lifted, Barton saw that two years had passed. The Christmas tree was there, but his father and mother had disappeared, lost forever at sea.

The butler tried to comfort the little boy by playing a melody on the violin. The maid gently stroked his head, while the cook offered him a freshly baked gingerbread man.

"NO!" shouted the boy. "I HATE CHRISTMAS."

In his hiding place in the wall, Barton felt a tear roll down his cheek. He wanted so much to console the little boy he had once been.

Dong. Dong. Dong ... the big clock continued to chime.

"Now here is the magic of Christmas Present," announced the little mouse.

Barton was surprised to see the shack where the homeless orphans lived. Sitting around a flickering fire of twigs, Lulu and her friends were singing as they roasted chestnuts.

They had decorated their shack with a holly wreath and anything else they could find to give it a festive air. But their meager feast and the rags they wore were pitiful to see.

Looking toward the mansion on the hill, one of the boys said, "That wretched Barton didn't even open his door when we went caroling there."

"He could have shared his food with us," added a little girl. "Or his toys. He won't play with anyone. He never shares anything with anybody."

Gently, Lulu told them they shouldn't speak
that way. She explained that Barton didn't have a
family either, and that he was surely sad. But while they
were lucky to have each other, he was all alone in his dreary mansion.
With a twinkle in her eyes, she went on:
"Merry Christmas, everyone. And Merry Christmas,
little orphan on the hill."

Dong. Dong. Dong ... struck the big clock.

"Now here is the magic of Christmas Yet to Come," said
the little mouse.

Barton slowly adjusted to the darkness that now filled
the mansion. By the light of a single candle, a tall young man
dressed in a nightshirt many sizes too small sat counting his
old toys over and over again.

"I was right to let the maid go, and the butler and the
cook," he grumbled. "I don't need them. I don't need anyone ...
not anyone at all."

Once again, mist enveloped the living room, and then
filled Barton's heart.

In the shack where the homeless orphans lived, there were no holly wreaths, nor was there a fire to roast chestnuts.

Lulu, stretched out on a bed of straw, lay shivering with fever. Her friends were gathered around, trying as best they could to keep her warm.

"If only we had wood to make a fire," one murmured.

"And food to give her strength … we have nothing to help her get better."

"NO," cried Barton as the mist gathered yet again. "NO! I don't want the future to be like this!"

Dong. Dong. Dong! rang out the last three strokes of midnight.

Barton opened his tear-filled eyes to see that he was back in his bed. He had returned to his normal size, and it was Christmas.

He jumped to his feet, rushed down the stairs and burst into the kitchen. The maid, the butler and the cook stared at him in wonder.

"It's time to celebrate!" shouted Barton joyfully. "Let's put up the decorations and prepare the feast! It's Christmas!"

Barton quickly pulled on his coat and ran out the door into the snowy night.

In the light-filled mansion, the magic of Christmas finally spread its wings. Seated around a table laden with delicious things to eat, the butler, the maid, the cook and all the children were singing merrily.

"What a wonderful Christmas!" exclaimed Lulu between mouthfuls.

"It's all thanks to you," answered Barton, his heart filled with happiness.

"It's thanks to all of you, my friends."

"My friends forever."

"Merry Christmas, little mouse.
Merry Christmas, everyone."